Agents
of
C.U.N.T.

Sonny Meadows

ISBN: **0692168257**
ISBN-13: **978-0692168257**

DEDICATION

This book is dedicated to Donald Trump, whose campaign and presidency caused me such deep confusion and dismay that I felt compelled to deal with it through this writing.

CONTENTS

ACKNOWLEDGMENTS

Deep gratitude to all the regulars at CK Cafe, formerly known as Nick's, fa'lettin me be myself.

1

Was just me and Joe tonight, or so I thought. Sitting at the bar and nursing a whiskey, I caught sight of a young woman entering alone from the corner of my eye. Without turning my head I swirled the ice as she sat two stools down from me. Her mouth remained closed, but the way she sidled up, the way she plopped her purse onto the bar, and the way she nudged her foot just a little further into her high heel shoe said pretty much everything. She needed something, and I happened to be able to provide it.

Joe came up to her, still wiping off a beer mug, then laid it aside. He rested his hand on the bar and, leaning in, let his eyes linger just a moment too long. "Feelin' like anything in particular tonight?"

"I been dying for a cocktail. Gimme' a Paloma."

He stroked his scraggly beard, his tongue licking the inside of his lip. "Comin' up."

As Joe mixed her drink, she turned to me and asked, "How are you?" I sensed danger. I used my finger to stir my drink, getting myself together. Raising my head, I looked at her for the first time. Wavy black hair, latina, she wore eyeglasses, but didn't need them to appear intelligent.

I asked her, "You ever hear the story of the greatest man who ever lived?"

She laughed through her reply, "No, please tell me."

"This man, and no, I don't mean Jesus, took a sad little boy with more questions than answers under his wing. He taught him, not with lectures and explanations, but by being an example of what a man should be. The boy went from being scared he might become bored with internet porn to banging cheerleaders while the rest of the squad jumped up and down waving their pom-poms." While I spoke, evenly and calmly, I observed her. The skin around her eyes tightened almost imperceptibly. Her mouth twitched into a nervous smile.

She replied, "I see."

I went back to nursing my whiskey. Joe laid her cocktail before her, but she didn't take a sip. I felt her fear, and waited.

"Sounds like this man taught you a lot."

The toilet in the bathroom across the room flushed and Jerry, my apprentice, emerged. Seeing the situation, he stopped as the door closed behind him, then went to sit at a table in the corner.

"He didn't teach me a thing," I said. "Because the man I'm referring to is me. Pleased to meet you, name's Barry... Barry Bonds." She knew the name, and well she should. Realizing too late that she had walked into the wrong bar, she shook her head, mouthing 'no' in terror as I continued, "But you should know that already, considering you're a cunt."

She grabbed her head, pulling her hair, trying in vain to hold in her screams. I sipped my whiskey, savoring the flavor, turning on my stool to face her as her eyes melted, dripping from their sockets and she rose, stumbling across the room and flailing as her insides liquefied and spewed out of her vagina. I almost felt bad for her as the pool of mess became silent. The last of her torso dripped out from inside her blouse, which lay along with the rest of her ensemble in the puddle where she had just been.

Joe let out a breath. "You think they're on to us?"

"Don't know. But this can't be a coincidence." I turned to Jerry, who'd never seen a cunt melting before. "Get over here and clean this up. I gotta' go talk to some people."

I exited the bar as Joe flipped the closed sign and

locked up behind me.

'*Have you ever seen the look of total peace upon the face of a terrorist as he's about to die? God is great.*'
The thought lingered in my mind, and I realized that it seemed to come from somewhere else. Somewhere outside of me. I stopped, standing, wary. Half expecting an enormous spider. But, no. Just people.

I continued for a couple blocks to the dojo, where an associate of mine taught young men martial arts as well as the arts of womanizing. I stopped outside the glass door of the unit, looking inside. There was nobody there. The room was mostly empty except for a floor mat where the students would line up and learn the practice of manipulating their chi into their testicles, making them impervious to punishment. I hadn't bothered learning this technique myself. It was too hokey and I simply avoided any situations where I might get kicked in the groin.

I turned to see an old lady with a beehive hairdo coming straight up to me. In an instant she lifted up her palm and blew into it, sending a cloud of pinkish dust right into my face.

I lost all feeling in my body, and my legs buckled. No longer able to sense my feet on the ground, I fell over. All I could see was the concrete of the sidewalk, and my mind swam until it seemed the crags and cracks of the concrete were all that had ever existed.

I heard her footsteps walking slowly away, her shoes clapping against the ground until the sound filling my ears was all that could ever be heard in the world.

I didn't want it to be this way, but I had to find a place to go. All I could feel was fear, and damned if I was gonna' shit right where I stood.

I was in the bakery, but I'd forgotten what I'd come for. There was certainty in the confusion. I knew I was about to die, and it was just as it should be.

I awoke. The toilet ran next to me like a broken fountain. I lifted my head. I was in the bakery, in the world. I felt no pain. No emotion. I turned the door handle and my hand could still touch it.

A woman sat at a table and I came up to her, feeling her shoulder. She flung her gaze in my direction as convulsions of relief went through me in waves.

A crowd gathered 'round and, as I was led away by cops, I let myself go with it.

Sitting in the police station I kept expecting someone to ask me if I was okay. No one did. People glided around me like they were living in a dream. A vague notion that there was something I should be doing about my situation was there, but I couldn't pay any attention to it. I had to get myself together, just enough to convince the cops I could walk outta' here.

I came to in a prison cell with the taste of semen in my mouth. A man snored, deep and loud, in the bunk beneath me, and I didn't want to wake him. I lifted my hand silently to feel my shirt, which had been tied around my head, the sleeves tightened into a little knot to hold it in place. I touched my lips, covered in makeup to make me pretty. I didn't feel pretty, and I felt like it was the asshole beneath me to blame.

I curled myself into a corner, dug my chin deep between my knees. All I knew was that morning would come.

Just as I was coming to terms with what was really important in life the lights to the cell block flickered on and a guard walked down the rows banging his stick against the bars. "Everybody up! Big day ahead..."

My bunk mate stretched and yawned himself awake. "Honey sweetie?" His gravelly voice was so irritating, I wanted to puke. "You awake?" I could hear him softly clapping his hands together. "Today's the day!" He leaned out of bed and popped up to gaze at me. "You ready?"

"What's today?" I asked.

He slammed his fist against the bed rail. "Today you become my number one fish, bitch! Don't you remember?" His feelings were clearly hurt. "You meant all those things you said, right?"

"There must be some mistake. I'm a ladies man, through and through."

He lowered his pants. "Do we have to do this all over again?"

The guard slammed his nightstick against the bars of the cell. "Ladies! Time for chow." A buzzer sounded and all the doors slid open. I jumped down, sauntering past the big man, swaying my hips, turning my head to face him as I went, "I could have any man in here. What makes you think I'd be with you?"

I could feel his stare at my back, like chiseled stone, as we walked in file to the mess. I took a tray, getting my food before he did, making eyes at the other prisoners. Not too much, just enough to let him know. My plan was to have him throwing punches at two or three of them by the time we got to the jello. A wiry white dude got up from a table and nudged the big man by his shoulder, turning him around. "Hey, looks like the fish is up for grabs. That so?"

I pretended to look shocked, "That's not true! Is it?"

"She don't look happy." The black guy on my other side wiped his mouth in anticipation.

"We're in a serious relationship, fella's." I made

myself look confused, "Though, truth be told our sex life has been a little stale lately."

The white dude got into his face. "There you have it, she says so herself."

"Darling, I'm not available, am I?" I gave my bunk mate the doe eyes, pleading with him.

He tried to reassure me, saying, "No! Of course not..." The black guy sucker punched him as a brawl broke out. Guards came running, but were quickly caught up in the mayhem.

By the time I had slipped out of the cafeteria, alarms were blaring throughout the prison. I sidestepped two guards in riot gear just before they turned a corner by slipping inside the laundry room.

Two laundry disposal drivers were loading big bins into the back of a truck. "Faster! Let's get the fuck outta' this hell hole." There was one bin left and as they loaded another I jumped in, piling linens over myself and laying deathly still.

I felt myself being loaded and heard the doors slam shut. In a moment we were headed out the gate.

Something had to be amiss. The big questions in life were yearning to be asked. *'Who am I?', 'How did I get here?'*, and the one I could actually answer, *'Where can I get some weed?'*

I crawled out of the laundry bin, waiting for the

truck to stop at a red light, and flung the doors open, running for my life towards Vinny's pad.

Sitting at her ancient oak desk on a throne once occupied by the line of King Louis, Lillith stroked the snow white fur of her Persian kitty. They purred as one, oblivious and indifferent. A handful of minions wearing leather bondage slave suits dusted and cleaned her antique shop. Their pot-bellies hung bare, jiggling over their otherwise exposed penises. Bi-focals rested low on her narrow nose and a gray bee-hive hair-do towered atop her skull. Her pasty white skin was wrinkled like fabric. A purple dress adorned with lilies and fleur-de-lis' hung draped over her knees down to her frilly white socks. Red shoes.

Agent Penny Hardaway sat across from her, wet from the dark feminine power permeating the room. Her dark legs were bare and strong below her purple mini-skirt and one of them crossed over her knee. Her dangling foot moved up and down with a subdued erotic energy, the toes stretching to point straight upward, and then relaxing in an irregular rhythm. Her dome shaped afro and large hoop earrings were immaculate.

Lillith purred, "The sacrifice of Suarez appears to have not been in vain."

Penny's head drooped, "She knew the risks when she joined C.U.N.T."

"Quite so." Lillith smiled at her kitty, "As did you. I want one more thing from you, Penny."

Penny tensed, "Anything."

"Its time we re-introduced ourselves to The Eunuch. With our biggest obstacle removed, I can clear out some detritus from the past."

"You know where he is?"

"I know how to find him. You will tail our latest victim," she glared in delight. "I feel strongly he will be finding The Eunuch for us."

"Of course."

Lillith screamed, "Do not fuck this up!" Then went back to her kitty. "This is personal."

One last place left. Back to the start. El Leche de Hombre was an anything goes kinda' club. Jerry had first run into Barry Bonds that night a year ago when he had flipped his laptop shut, determined to leave internet porn behind, and had crept into line outside this building just off the red light district.

Nearly certain the one slouched at the bar had been female, he had come up behind her and, with a crackle in his voice, asked her what her name was. She had turned, smiled, looked Jerry up and down, got up and walked away, saying, "You're not ready for that information."

He had sat, holding back loser tears, when Barry came up, introducing himself. Jerry turned to face him, and as they had talked Jerry could almost feel Barry portraying himself, showing Jerry a performance to reveal what he could be. It was like watching the performance of a reflection in the mirror where the image in the reflection was of someone other than oneself.

By the time that night had ended he had had to find his way home from a strange woman's apartment with her scent wafting behind him the whole way.

Freaks surrounded him now, just as they had. Garishly colored hair-dos. Leather suits. Strap-on fashion accessories. The whole nine yards. That first night he had been frightened. Now he was scared, but not for himself- if he was unable to find Barry here, he wouldn't be found.

The packed club had go-go dancers mounted on the walls, sitting on toilets and stroking large black dildos. Near the ceiling, monkeys in cages threw poop onto the crowd below, their eerie calls nearly drowned out in the din. Jerry wandered into one of the side rooms, where people lounged on long couches sucking and fucking whatever was near.

Going from couch to couch, he flashed a photo of Barry on his me-phone, asking, "Have you seen this man?" With grunts, nods, and annoyed looks it was clear he was getting nowhere. He entered the main room to see security, dressed in their gorilla suits, headed his way, struggling to weave though the crowd from across the club.

"That's Barry." Jerry jerked his head. It was her, and he gazed.

"You have an Adam's apple."

"Yah. I know."

The buzz of the crowd lifted in his mind. Jerry's focus remained fixed on her throat. "I never noticed it before."

"Do I know you?"

He held up his me-phone. "You know where Barry is?"

She retreated a step. "What did he do?"

"Nothing, he's been missing."

"I'm sorry to hear that. He still owes me two hundred for letting that timid boy fist my asshole last year."

"That was me!" He smiled at her. "I'm the one who anal fisted you."

She peered close. "Huh! How ya' doin'?"

A gorilla grabbed Jerry's shoulder, shoving him aside and then pushed him roughly through the crowd and into the rear exit, bashing him against the bar door-handle and out, sending him diving head first into the alley. The gorilla pointed, "No pictures!" He lifted a walkie-talkie, pressing the button. He announced, "Got the pervert, over," and went back inside, letting the door shut itself with a click.

Jerry lifted himself to his feet and ran over to the door, pounding on its metal and yelling, "Fuck you!", over and over. In a few moments he was spent, and turned his back against the door, letting himself slide down to a sitting position.

Someone down the alleyway groaned from behind a dumpster. Jerry looked to see a pair of feet, one with a pink sock covered in little yellow ducks, and the other bare and filthy, sticking out. He rose and stepped gingerly over, his shoes scraping lightly against the concrete.

Looking down, a man was laid out on the ground with just plain blue pants and no shirt. Hypodermic needles were scattered around and on him, one still sticking into his arm. White flakes speckled his chin that were maybe crack, or maybe jizz. He looked closer, it was both.

He looked familiar. '*Is it...?*' "It is!" Jerry leaned down, lightly slapping Barry's face. "Barry! Wake up!"

Barry grunted and shoo 'ed Jerry away with a flick of his wrist.

"What happened to you?"

A woman giggled. Jerry looked to see her silhouette standing at the entrance of the alleyway. She lingered a moment, then slipped away, vanishing into the city night.

Jerry hesitated, almost needing to run after her. Barry shifted onto his side, nestling his head onto his hands in slumber, and Jerry reached out to lift him up, saying, "No, come on. Get up."

2

Things were looking up. A man lifted me to my feet, looking for a Thursday night milkshake. I let him know I was happy to oblige, yet he insisted on showing me respect despite my protestations. He led me away to his car, which was a nice red Honda, and I determined I would give him something gratis. He was nice, he had soft skin and when I asked, he said his car was paid for.

He took me to a bar, introducing me to the bartender. Feeling a threesome coming down the pipe, I waited, giving eyes to the two men playing pool across the room. No one bit.

Finally I yelled, "Whose dick I gotta' suck to get a drink around here?!" These men clearly didn't know how to treat a lady, and I wasn't gonna' stand for it.

They handed me a bottle, getting me drunk. I was down. I found myself guzzling in a back room, two men standing in front of me. I knew what was coming.

I woke up and it was morning. I reached back and felt my asshole. Nothing. Suddenly, I didn't trust these people.

Behind the bar, Joe leaned his head way back, gulping down a shot. Jerry pleaded with him, "You said this Eunuch might be able to help!"

"Forget it, kid. The Eunuch used to be a ladies man extraordinaire, I mean movie stars, princesses, hell... queens! Then, one day he decides to chop off his own balls. Said it would give him some sort of magical powers. These days he sits around in a secret apartment, surrounded by arcane objects and knitting sweaters."

"You know where he is, don't you?"

Joe slammed the shot glass down. "Did you see Barry!? Is that even him anymore? It sucks, kid, but you gotta' let it go. Now shut up about it or I'll fuck your mom."

Jerry saw. "Guess I'll be on my way, then."

"Take that tart in the office with you!"

Barry had found another bottle and was far from shore as Jerry took him by the elbow and led him to his place.

The following weeks went by in a haze. Having quit on giving a fuck about anything, Jerry drowned himself in pussy. The 'plan' was fucking every hole possible until the sweet release of merciful death. Lonely women, wealthy women, street dwellers, college chicks... he took on all comers.

Meanwhile, I had taken to re-decorating Jerry's apartment. One night Jerry had brought home a 'cute-as-fuck Asian chick', as he had put it, to find I had re-arranged his furniture in order to create more flow and space.

After banging in the bedroom, Jerry walked out and I confronted him. "Jerry, I feel you're trying to fill an emotional void, and you've been neglecting my needs."

"Fuck your needs, bitch."

That was a mean thing to say, but I took a breath and continued. It was time I let him know there was another man in my life. "I've been talking with someone, and he's made me realize I'm worth more than you've been giving me credit for."

"What!? Who've you been talking with?"

"Oh, every day we meet in Rosa Park and talk. He just listens. I just love that he has no interest in tearing me up, you see, he's what people call a eunuch."

"You know what... I don't care. Go to this eunuch. Get out."

"I'm picking up just a little resentment..."

"Get the fuck out!"

"Alright, Jerry." I walked to the door. I had someone better to go to. Just before exiting, I turned to him, saying, "I hope you can find happiness."

The Asian chick peeped her head out from inside the bedroom. "Is this a bad time?"

"No! Its a fucking great time!"

"I can't find my panties."

"Well, maybe if you looked underneath the dresser, where I tossed them, you'd find them, okay?"

She muttered *asshole* beneath her breath as she went back inside the bedroom. Jerry grabbed a beer from the fridge as she re-emerged, heading straight for the front door.

Jerry swigged as the door slammed behind her.

Sitting on a bench near the fountain with a statue of a nymph pissing on a frog, I knew The Eunuch would be along shortly. He never called, or made contact in any way but, somehow, The Eunuch always knew when I would be there, and The Eunuch never failed to arrive.

A small child came up to me, gazing into my eyes, and I felt uncomfortable. The child's mother came running up from behind me, "I'm sorry!" She was in her early thirties, wearing jeans and dainty sneakers. She bent over to pick up her child and breasts swelled from beneath her blouse, which hung loose around her cleavage. "Turn your head for a second," she remarked, smiling. "Come on," she cooed, leading her child away.

"What did you just notice?"

I looked to my side, startled. The Eunuch sat beside me with his bald white scalp glinting in the springtime. He was in a cream-colored suit which hung casual and loose like the wrinkles on his face. His legs were crossed like a European and brown leather loafers fit his feet like a second pair of skin.

"A child. And a mother," I said.

The Eunuch poked a little straw into a juice box, taking a sip. "Look deeper. What did you just see?"

"I was uncomfortable, with the promise of new life... and then she bent over, and..."

"Yes? What did you see?"

"Boobies."

"That's right." The Eunuch offered me some juice, but I waved it away.

"They were nice."

"Nice?"

"No. What am I saying, they were magnificent."

"You got it." The Eunuch sipped from his juice box. "What do you remember about yourself?"

I tried to think, but I couldn't remember anything before my run-in with the boy I'd been staying with.

"Would you like to see those boobies again?"

"Yes."

"Perhaps, see her naked?"

"I would." I began to shake, nearly jumping off the bench in a fit. "What do I do?"

"Remember."

A calm came over me. I stood, taking in the scene and letting out a breath, then I went over to the mother.

The Eunuch observed from the bench, sipping, as I chatted up the mother. I laughed. The mother laughed. I made the child smile. I whispered something to her, and she blushed. I held her by the waist, softly saying something, then stepped back. I looked over to see The Eunuch's heart filling with pride as the mother looked around to see if anyone was looking before lifting her blouse and flashing a magnificent pair of boobies. I mouthed the words, 'Thank you', and kissed her goodbye, just a peck on the cheek before going back over to the bench.

The Eunuch remained in silence while the sounds of the park permeated the air. I sat, taking it all in. "I remember who I am."

"Are you ready?"

I looked him in the eye, smiling. "Oh yeah, I'm

ready."

Sipping the last of the juice with a slurp, The Eunuch crushed the box in his hand and tossed it into the trash. "You can call me Martin. Now let's go."

Standing by the fence at the basketball court, Agent Penny Hardaway watched Barry leaving with The Eunuch. She had orders not to interfere, and whatever Lillith was thinking she couldn't fathom. Her finger caressed a plastic baggie full of special cookies. Behind her, men played a pick-up game, the sounds of grunts and shouts, the ball bouncing on tarmac, and clanging against the rim. Then the court fell silent, and she turned to see the local basketball star coming towards her, the ball snug between his hand and his hip.

"Hey girl, hey!"

She faced him. "What you want?"

"You see me school these fools? Name's Smoove. What's yours?"

"I didn't notice." She turned away, seeing Barry and The Eunuch heading towards a limousine. "Name's Cookie. I make the special-est cookies around." She held up her baggie. "You want one?"

"Damn! My favorite. How much?"

"Tell you what... You and me, one-on-one, you win you get all these cookies."

The other men groaned, some putting their hands to their mouths. "Oh! Damn, Smoove, you gonna' share those with us?"

Smoove bounced the ball to Penny. "You're on."

"First one to five. I got places to be."

Penny moved like a panther, dribbling between her legs, then through Smoove's legs while spinning around him to catch the ball and she jumped, soaring through the air to slam it home.

Astonished, the men became silent. "Alright." Smoove took the ball. "Not bad."

Smoove dribbled behind his back. He faked left, went right, but Penny poked her hand in and tapped the ball away as Smoove ran for the basket. She sauntered over and picked it up. Without taking a step she launched a three, and stared Smoove down as it swished through the net.

She tossed Smoove the baggie, "No hard feelings." She walked off the court as the other men swiped the baggie from Smoove, tearing it open and munching.

As the limousine pulled away, she went to her car and got in, muttering, "So fucking typical."

Behind her the men choked in fits, falling to the court in convulsions and spewing cookie-filled vomit.

3

"Bad words have true power. When someone hears a bad word, all illusion of choice, of free-will, of any possibility for peace of mind- that mental refuge of the weak, vanishes, and its as if I, who simply utters them, am master of reality."

Hearing the man speak, I had to admit, it made sense. My mind seemed to be returning, and the fugue state, with its dream-like quality, faded into nothing. "Cunt." I said it, as if in communion. I sat across from him as he lounged on a settee, his feet resting on a table with arcane tomes piled neatly. His apartment had all the trappings of a lair. I felt as if I had stepped inside a sacred space where both cynicism and confusion were nurtured.

"That's a special word." He crossed his legs, he exuded ease, and he rested his hands on his knee. "Don't waste your breath. You say that word, and direct it towards just the right person, you steal everything they have... ever had, and yes, everything they ever will have. Its, perhaps, the most useful weapon at our disposal." Taking a moment to peer over to his wall, which had all sorts of magical talismans in glass cases, he considered the best course. "However, it won't be enough to achieve our total victory."

I felt as though I should speak, but nothing came to mind. He continued, "Lillith's designs are potent. She's close to something... Should she succeed, we're, how shall I say? Burnt toast. Does that make sense?"

"Crystal."

He rose, going over to his cases. "Good." He opened a lid, surveying his arsenal. "We will need allies in this fight." Taking an old and warped piece of round metal, he carefully strung a thin leather strap though a hole near its edge. He placed it around his neck, hiding it beneath his shirt, then turned to me. "We're going to Boro Park."

Penny's orders were to arrive at a secret location which had no address. She followed the directions which had been downloaded onto her me-phone, the voice telling her to turn left between two abandoned warehouses. It seemed to be a dead end as she drove between two haphazardly positioned dumpsters, then the voice on her me-phone told her that she had arrived. She pulled up to park, seeing Tiffany standing next to a pink Corvette and snuggling a tiny dog in her arms. Penny rolled up her windows, not wanting that blonde bimbo's smelly twat to stink up her interior.

"Nice car, you trade it for food stamps?"

"Hey, Tiffany. Saw your sex tape... at least up until the boring part. You know, where you started having sex?"

A car crashed into a dumpster, sending it sliding into the opposite wall. They jerked their heads around to see Suzuki pulling up in her Mazda, scraping another dumpster before backing up again and smashing into the warehouse. She opened her door, the bent metal creaking and snapping open with a loud 'pop'. She tossed a half-eaten container of noodles and chopsticks onto the ground before getting out. She hurried over to the other girls. "I miss anything?"

"Yeah, Tiffany took one in the ass..."

Suzuki giggled, "No, I saw that already."

Tiffany pulled on the skin around her eyes, making them squinty. "Oh, yoo sawr ih aourleady, Suzuki?" Suzuki drooped visibly, holding in a tear and, seeing this, Tiffany pretended to rub her eyes with her fists. "Awl wee clying?"

Suzuki let go of the act, looking straight at Tiffany.

"Nah. I'm good."

Penny laughed, "Racist white bitch."

Tiffany took out her me-phone, "What was your bosses name again, Penny?" She started to dial. "Carlos? When he hears how you fucked his wife, bitch, you are so fired."

Penny stepped forward, "Fuck you, Tiffany."

"Bitch," Tiffany hissed while dialing, then put the me-phone to her ear.

Suzuki had been waving for them to shut up, "Hey, girls?"

They turned to see Ronda standing behind them, her thighs sturdy like oak stumps. Tiffany pasted on a smile, "Ronda! I'm so glad you're here too. We were just keeping our wits sharp, you know, for the big fight."

Ronda stepped up and put her horse face into Tiffany's grill. "I'm not here to train you stupid hoes anymore. Lillith is waiting inside."

They entered into a vast space, the warehouse empty except for an unconscious man strapped to a table which was angled upward in order for Lillith, who stood before him, to have a better view of his suffering. The Persian kitty moved around the table, lapping from the blood pooling around a drain on the hard floor, red ooze staining its pure white whiskers and dainty paws.

The agents gathered around like felines, engaged with the pleasure of their conquest.

"Who's the mouse?" Suzuki contained her excitement. "Can I kill him?"

"His name is Jerry, or so I'm told."

"What's he for?" Tiffany feigned boredom. "Wouldn't he be more fun with some false hope? Like an unloaded gun or something?"

Jerry stirred, moving his head and gasping in pain. He kept his eyes shut tight, not wanting to face it. Over nine hundred small cuts covered his body, Lillith having adorned him with a scalpel. She held it out, stepping towards him, and as if able to sense the impending torture, he squirmed in slow agony. She hovered her scalpel over his thigh, silently, without a whisper, and Jerry jerked his eyes open in panic. "Stop! Please!" He pleaded, "What do you want!?" In disbelief, he repeated the only words he knew that might save him, "I told you, I know where Barry is... I can help you find The Eunuch...", his voice finally trailing off into despair.

As the cut came, he quivered in acceptance.

Lillith soothed, "Try not to over-think this, we're just having a little fun."

Jerry turned his head to rest, and a breath, barely a sigh, escaped him as he died.

"Nine hundred and twelve. Over five thousand years I've been doing this, and not once has someone made it to a thousand." She stepped over to address them. "Once a man made it to nine hundred eighty nine."

Her eyes twinkled. "That was fun."

"I can smell your pussy from here, Lillith." I said it to myself. I felt so very close, and it was good to be on the offensive again as we made our way through a Boro Park alley.

"Ease up there, amigo, that thing wouldn't be caught dead around this neighborhood." The Eunuch, or Martin as I'd begun calling him, led the way. "Its best we keep off the main thoroughfares. Don't want to run into any rabbis." He kept his head on a swivel, looking out for any potential threats. "At least not yet."

"Where we headed?"

He just kept walking, so I stopped. "Look, I may be along for this ride, but you gotta' let me in on the goings on or I just might find my own way to bag that lady monster."

Martin gasped, facing me. "Okay, you know the Queen of the Jews?"

Nope. "Never heard of her."

"Exactly. So get in line like a good little duckling or, yes, you can find your own way to... 'bag' her." He resumed the pace, like he already knew what I'd do about it. He was right, and I followed.

A quiet scrape on the ground came from behind me. Without looking, I sped up until I was astride with Martin. "You hear that?", I said beneath my breath.

He didn't bother to lower his voice, "We're being followed." He kept the pace. "Come on, we'll never arrive if we stop to chat."

In front of us an orthodox rabbi stepped out from behind a stack of crates. He stood firm, facing us down, his hands hanging loose by his side.

Martin stopped. "Ah, shitballs." We both looked behind us to see two more rabbis appear from the recesses. Martin turned back around to face the first guy. I kept one eye on the other two. With his palm outstretched, Martin commanded, "Take me to your Queen!"

The rabbi laughed. He removed his black hat and tossed it, brim down, onto the ground at his feet. His curly sideburns swayed like charms on a chain. "Forget it. This is as far as you go."

I noticed the other two were doing the same thing and, despite being able to handle myself, I couldn't help but feel that I was about to get a beating.

Martin whispered. "Alright, don't swing for where they're at. Swing for where they're going to be."

Before that nonsense had time to sink in I felt a fist slam into my neck. I turned to catch a glimpse of a rabbi, and I swung. He vanished, and I caught nothing but air. Another fist smashed the side of my face. I screamed out, "Goddamnit!", throwing a wild haymaker to the side. There was no one there.

Martin shot lightning bolts from his fingers, moving his hands to aim at a rabbi who was sprinting by. When his target vanished there was nothing but a seared brick wall.

We stood back to back. Breathing hard. No sign of any rabbis.

"Close your eyes, Barry." Martin whispered, "When you feel a wisp of breeze, swing behind you."

"Shit." Just what I needed, really bad advice. I shut my eyes tight.

"Relax. Wait for it."

I breathed, feeling the tension. A breeze ruffled my hair...

The impact was beautiful. His jaw gave into me like a Mormon girl getting offa' meth.

Martin ducked to the side, firing behind me and a rabbi flew into a dumpster, his black coat smoking.

The rabbi at my feet groaned, trying to get up, and I leaned in, grunting and kicking him in the ribs.

"Enough!" Martin put his hand out to stop me, then turned to address the emptiness along the alleyway. "We come as friends!"

A voice echoed, "Friends! I've got friends, none of them look like you."

"Do any of them know how to find Lillith?"

Quiet. The two injured rabbis got to their feet and

retreated in opposite directions, looking back at us with wary eyes before disappearing behind over-stuffed garbage cans.

Moments passed. "What now?", I asked.

"We wait."

4

Padme had a cooking show, so she knew a good meatball, and this was a damn good meatball. Also, Natalie Portman was stuffing her pie-hole across the table, slurping long strands of saucy noodles and grunting in satisfaction. Natalie looked up from her plate, giving Padme the thumbs up, and her me-phone jingled a Harry Connick Jr. tune. "Mmm, this shit is so good. Excuse me." She answered, "Natalie Portman."

The tone of the hushed 'wawa' voice emitting from the me-phone, and the concern crossing Natalie's face alerted Padme, and she picked up a dish and carried it over to the sink.

Natalie listened, then laid into the caller, "Why are you even questioning me? No! Tell that ball-less hocus-pocus freak to go fuck himself with his non-existent erection." She hung up the me-phone. "Sorry, Padme. People, I tell ya'." She brought her dishes over.

"Just leave it. I'll take care of them."

Natalie placed her dishes on the counter, gripping them, her knuckles turning white in anger and frustration. She turned, then uttered a shrill scream and whipped her wine glass through the air and against the cabinets. Pieces shattered, raining all over the kitchen. She rested her hand on her forehead, gathering herself. "Sorry, I'm sorry, I just..."

"Okay, calm yourself. You need to breathe..."

"Its these fucking rabbis! I can't eat a plate of spaghetti without some mythical being from ancient folklore popping up outta' nowhere and..." She waved her hands around, flustered.

"Okay, okay. Tell me the problem."

"Its Lillith. She's in town, and the rabbis want me to meet this... guy, who they say can maybe lead them straight to her."

"Lillith is a monster, Natalie. If there's even a chance... you gotta' at least try."

Natalie grimaced, in a cute way, and relented with a chuckle. "Oh... You're right."

"Of course I am."

"I'll take the meeting."

Padme lifted a spoon full of chocolate ice cream, smirking. "After dessert."

Tiffany looked through the scope, all the way along 9th Avenue and down into Fred's Diner. Martin sipped coffee while the jerk pushed his fork through a slice of pie. She felt an itch, and scratched herself just below her breast. "Pieces of shit," she sneered under her breath.

A woman in a cute little dress entered the diner and sat herself at the table in front of them. Her shoes were a little tacky and she was blocking the view, so Tiffany looked up from her scope and checked to see where Shitzy was. He lay in the corner, licking his lips in contentedness.

"Is she hot?" I'd always kinda liked the idea of bagging a queen.

"Oh," Martin sipped his tea. "Hot enough, I suppose. Oddly enough I fucked her mother, back before the whole castration thing."

"Nice." The pie was still warm. Cherry and tasty, like I bet The Queen was. "When we meet her?"

"Soon, I hope. If she agrees, one of the rabbi's will approach us. If not..."

"What, why wouldn't she?"

"She's self-absorbed and can be quite judgy."

"I like it. So, if she doesn't agree, what then?"

"We sneak into her apartment and command her attention."

I was about to offer ideas about how best to get into her place when a rabbi came in the door. I glanced, then kept my eyes down. "Don't look now..."

Martin raised his cup to his lips, "Its a rabbi. I can sense them." The rabbi sat at the counter, perusing a menu.

I wasn't in the mood for waiting around anymore, so as Martin was saying something I got up and walked over, tapping him on the shoulder. He turned. "Any word from your Queen?"

He turned again to face forward, closing the menu and placing it aside. Without looking at me he said, "Please return to your seat and enjoy your food. She'll arrive shortly."

I did as he asked, sitting and giving a nod to Martin. He looked pleased.

I looked out the window, down 9th. No sign of any queens, but a woman walked up and entered. "Who's that?"

Martin turned to see. "I don't know."

Imagine my luck when she came straight over. She stood in a brown trench coat, regarding us. What I could see of her legs told me they were strong and, also she was smokin' hot.

She stood, saying nothing, so I spoke up, "Hey, you gonna' stand there, or you gonna' dance?"

Before I knew it, she grabbed my full hair and lifted me outta' my seat. I still didn't know what was goin' on when I was bent over the table with my forearm being jammed hard into my back. She leaned down and whispered in my ear, all sexy like, "Lick my pussy, asshole."

I was at a loss, so I gave in. "Okay," I said and she let me go.

I tried to rub the pain outta' my arm. It wasn't helping. "Name's Barry Bonds, who are you?"

"That's not important, you two must come with me, now. Your lives may depend on it."

Far be it for me to turn down an offer from a pretty lady. "Sure." I turned to Martin. "Come on."

"Wait!" Martin didn't know a good thing when it slapped him in the face, and he tried to pull me back as I followed the mystery woman out the door.

As we were leaving I coulda' swore I saw Natalie Portman coming down the street. I peered, and as she approached I saw that it was her alright.

Natalie Portman walked up. She had a thin smile and was about to shake Martin's hand when her brains splattered all over the cafe window. Some got on the shoulder of his coat too, but with no time to wipe it off with a napkin, he ducked behind a car.

The mystery woman moved quick, grabbing my good arm and dragging me inside the cafe. We took cover behind the counter, next to the rabbi. "Looks like the Queen is dead, rabbi."

He shook in fear. "Its those demons sent by Lillith!" The other patrons were all whimpering and writing letters to their former selves saying things like how they were sorry for all the easy choices they had taken and that they had never asked that person out. "I have to get out there and save her."

"Don't do that, I got some brains on my sleeve here."

He wailed, standing and just as he took a step his brains sprayed the floor behind him. Shrieks from the patrons made it hard to think.

I turned to the woman, who had been busy scoping possible exits. "Any good ideas, sweety?"

"Don't worry, I'll get us out of this. Follow me."

She crawled her way along the counter, and I followed. Her ass swayed like the ocean on a moonlit night, and I quickened my pace to get close enough to sniff her pussy. The rabbi's brains were slimy and made it difficult to move.

We crawled into the kitchen and through a door into the alleyway, then ran to the street where a black car waited. The rear door opened as we came up and she shoved me inside. She got in and the car took off down the street.

I puked in my mouth as the city blurred through the windows. I looked to my left. The mystery woman was stroking her pussy fur with the cold hard steel of a revolver and the man in the passenger seat looked at me over his shoulder. I saw that he had a mouth on his forehead. This mouth grinned at me, like it knew something I didn't, and that this knowledge would kill me. His regular mouth spoke, "Watch out for republicans. They'll be popping outta' nowhere." His voice was soothing, like he knew just what he was saying. "Evil hides inside them."

I swallowed. There were chunks of burrito too large to enjoy, so I chewed them into paste. A total certainty overwhelmed me, and all that had been became the realization that I would never again awaken, and my mind shuddered, still clinging, never letting go of the reality that I am incapable of sleep. I needed to black out, and I peered out the window, upwards at the buildings. Spider things with tentacle legs and beaks scurried into a particular space in the sky, pouring in, crawling all over the puffs of clouds. "Do you see this?" I asked, fully expecting the words to sound like gibberish.

"We see it, Mr. Bonds." As the mystery woman spoke, I knew it was true, and when I turned to her there was total sense. She regarded me, holding a syringe in her hand.

Satisfied, she nodded to the men up front. The driver turned the ignition, pulling away from a parking lot next to the river, where we had apparently been parked. I rode in silence.

"How do you feel?" She asked me. The tires on the street soothed my journey, like tangible notions. I replied with a tiny breath, barely a groan. "You need rest," she said, and told the driver, "Dan, take us to the safe house."

Finally, I crawled into a bed.

5

The room was quiet. Someone ran the faucet and a cup clinked against the counter. I opened my eyes.

A man made coffee. It seemed he was alone here, but his shoulders drooped and his feet dragged from hours of wakeful exhaustion. He had been watching over me, and my eyes closed again.

In a dreamlike state I felt a burning in my shoulders. At first, I became aware of the hopes and dreams of everyone I'd ever known. Then, almost impossibly, I felt the fears of everyone I'd ever know. As this awareness, which felt like a more real sort of love, spread to include the other people I only knew through connection, I opened my eyes in a panic, and a ceiling fan spun over my head.

As it turned I could see its fans in motion with clarity. The sounds it made were too precise to be rhythmic. They were simply repetitive. A subtle notion flashed through me that I had to learn to enjoy and appreciate this sort of motion.

"He's awake." She spoke to me.

She sat in a chair, separate from the rest of the room, staying by my side.

"What happened?," I asked her.

"We injected you with some very powerful stuff, Mr. Bonds."

"What's your name?," I asked, and a hint of a smile appeared on her face.

"Lilly."

I took a moment. "I had an aunt with that name."

"Can you stand?"

I knew. "Of course." I tossed the covers aside and, my clothes drenched in sweat, arose. "What now?"

She stood, going over to get a coffee mug. "That is uncertain."

The man who had been in the room before came in through the door, alarmed. "We need to go."

"Already?" She handed me a pistol. "You know how to use one of these?"

"Think I saw it in the movies once." I reached for it, and she jerked it back. "I'll take that as a 'no'. Stay close to me."

The man who had been driving waited in the other room. "Let's go."

We filed through the door and out into an abandoned section of the city. A homeless man sat on the sidewalk nearby, leaning against a building. Dan went over to him, placing a bill into his outstretched hand. "Thanks, buddy." We got into the car.

We pulled away and Lilly told me, "You know Lillith... She doesn't have it in for you, its not personal."

"What do you know about it?"

She lowered her eyes, perhaps thinking what to say. "She's my mother."

"I'm sorry." It just came out. I didn't think, and I looked out the window, bearing the awkwardness. She said nothing.

Driving back to headquarters, Tiffany had to come up with a cover story for how she let those jerks and Lillith's daughter escape. That twat daughter wasn't even supposed to be there, and she nailed Natalie Portman through the head anyways, so what was the big deal? That was her best shot. Maybe Lillith wouldn't snap her wrists. She practiced her smile in the rear view mirror.

Pulling up to the parking lot behind the antique store, she found Penny standing by the rear entrance, smoking a cigarette. Tiffany got out of her 'vette, and Penny said, "Oooh, girl. You're in trooouble."

"Shut up!" She walked past Penny, into the store, and Penny followed her, not wanting to miss this.

She found Lillith sitting on her throne with her feet up, a minion painting her toe-nails pink. Suzuki stood by a bookshelf, texting some guy.

Lillith, still relaxing for her pedicure, said, "Tiffany, so nice you could make it."

"Lillith, they were right in my sights. How was I supposed to know Lilly would show up?"

Lillith jerked her eyes open. She shooed her minion away, sitting up in her throne. "Lilly was there?"

"She just appeared outta' nowhere. There was nothing I could do."

"How interesting. Fortunately, I have Suzuki." Suzuki put her me-phone away, smiling. "At least she never fails me." Lillith stood, going to stand between the two agents. She turned to Suzuki, putting her back to Tiffany. "I have a mission for you. Find The Eunuch and eliminate him. If you encounter Lilly, take her alive, if possible, and if not, dead will do. Either way, bring her to me."

Suzuki put her chest out with pride. "Consider it done."

Lillith went back and sat in her throne, putting her toes out for her minion. "I'm leaving for awhile. I have an important meeting with some very powerful people to attend. I expect this problem solved by the time I get back."

Dan stopped near the corner of 5th and Wallace. I asked what was going on, and Lilly turned to me, saying, "We're about to have our first date. Let's go get some cash."

I got out and ran across the street to catch up with her. She walked into the First Federal Bank, catching the revolving door in her stride. I entered the door and went through to see her pull out a handgun and fire it into the ceiling.

"Everyone get the fuck down on the floor! I only got enough bullets for eight of ya', and that doesn't make me happy..."

She aimed at the security guard, who froze, and she went over to him, taking his pistol from the holster. She looked at me. "You wanna' make yourself useful?"

I nodded my head and she tossed the gun into my hands. I held it for a moment, and then waved it around, saying. "I got at least five bullets! If my calculations are correct, some of you may live through this."

Lilly was already grabbing bags of cash from the tellers. I fired a round at the chandelier, and Lilly jerked her gaze at me. "I'm having fun!" She shook her head disapprovingly, grabbing the last bag and heading for the exit. I followed behind her, saying, "What are we doing next?"

As we got back into the car and raced away she said, "Alright, let's go get some supplies. We're going to the Tardo Mart.

The guy in the passenger seat had gotten himself some Cheasety-Ohs while we had been in the bank, and he decided he would stay in the car while the rest of us went shopping.

We went in to the wave of screeches from children in strollers, going past the young man standing on crutches, missing a leg, and with downs syndrome who greeted us with a warm smile, "Welcome to Tardo Mart."

"Gun section's in the back, get us some canned corn and stuff. We'll meet back at the checkout."

"What do I do?", I asked.

"Try to keep your sanity."

They went off on their missions, leaving me standing next to a pot bellied man in a MacDonalds cap. I could tell he didn't even work at MacDonalds. Over his shoulder I could see actual MacDonalds workers working at MacDonalds, and their uniforms were nothing like the airbrushed bald eagle and American flag on this guy's tee-shirt.

The man stood staring at a screen which displayed the MacDonalds logo and flashed news blurbs while viral videos played. The news blurbs said things like, 'Florida man says freedom used to be real', or 'woman from Newton wonders what she ever did'.

I wandered aimlessly, down aisles, past families

and other people who lived in their cars parked outside. As I weaved through and around, brushing against belly fat and bracing against random snippets of conversation, I felt a pain in my knee. It started dull and achy, slowly sharpening until my steps turned into a shuffle. The words I was hearing from the people around me seemed to echo like they were dropping into a pool of soft pity.

Then a woman's voice sounded over the inter-comm throughout the store. "Attention Tardo shoppers, find your way to aisle five." Her voice exuded excitement, and the people turned their heads to the ceiling, to where the voice was coming from. "Half-off Blackface Hillary dolls! Go get 'er!"

I looked. Right before me was the display of Blackface Hillary blow up dolls. The crinkled and dented cardboard boxes had images of Hillary Clinton in blackface, and her mouth was wide open in an 'oh' shape with a little jagged word bubble next to her that read, 'With real black lips!'.

The people nearby were shuffling in my direction, so I turned, only to see a herd coming down the other end of the aisle, shouting, "Get 'er!" and, "Fuck that bitch!".

I grabbed a doll and ran, only managing to limp quickly before the crowd took hold of me. The cries of children and shouts of anger made me wince, and meaty hands brushed against my face and pulled at my shoulders as they strained to take my box.

I managed to drop to the floor in fetal position as automatic gunfire sprayed the aisle. Arteries pierced and bellies exploded, spurting and oozing blood all over the floor. I peeked to see a man standing, raising his hands high and bellowing before a shotgun blast turned his chest into ground beef.

The woman's voice came over the inter-comm, "Thoughts and prayers...", ending with a scratch and a click before repeating on an endless loop, "Thoughts and prayers... Thoughts and prayers..."

I remained down, clinging to my toy, whimpering. I heard Dan say, "Should we leave him here?"

Lilly kneeled down, touching my shoulder. "Let it go, Barry."

I looked at her, seeing no pity, and I regarded the Blackface Hillary box. I dropped it, getting to my feet, and with the voice still looping we stepped over the carnage and back to the car.

We arrived back to see the man in the passenger seat hanging out the side window, limp and with a pool of blood on the concrete ground, dripping from his slit neck. Dan opened the door and pulled his body out to slump onto the parking lot.

"Come on," Lilly said, "We gotta' keep moving."

I regarded the man laying dead a moment. "Bye," I said, "I barely knew ya'". They loaded the trunk with ammo and weapons; an AK-47, a shotgun, several handguns, and a rocket launcher. I got in the passenger seat and we pulled away.

6

Martin sensed that Barry was headed west, but as he drove for hours the fatigue was weighing heavy on his brain, so he decided to stop at a hotel for the night and resume his search in the morning.

He got ready for bed, turning on the television to a romantic comedy and getting into his blue silk pajamas. After brushing his teeth and opening the sliding door to the outside balcony to get some fresh air, he got under the covers, sitting up against the wall and watching.

Tom Hanks ran across a suspension bridge, towards Meg Ryan. He'd seen this one before, but for some reason he didn't fully understand, as they came together, kissing on the bridge over the bay, he felt a deep sadness. He regretted so much that tears came welling up in his eyes. As he sobbed lightly, he took the remote and shut off the television, laying himself down and putting his cheek on the pillow. Closing his eyes, he tried to forget.

The meeting place had been set in an abandoned car repair shop. Lillith entered, followed by a single minion, to see Vinny Vitale, the big boss of the Cosa Nostra, and The Dragon Lady, who ran the biggest crime syndicate in China, already standing next to a hydraulic lift. Vinny had a large bodyguard dressed in a tailored suit and The Dragon Lady had a dangerous looking young man by her side.

Lillith approached them, saying, "Good of you to come." She came up to Vinny, taking his hand and kissing him on the cheek. "Vinny, how's the old lady?"

"Still crackin' heads, Lillith. Good to see you."

Lillith turned to The Dragon Lady and, in Mandarin, said with a slight bow of her head, "You are most respectfully welcome."

The old lady returned the bow and said in English, "May our coming together be beneficial to us both."

Lillith looked around, asking, "Where's Mastermind?"

"I'm right here!" Mastermind entered from the rear, his gray suit and bald head becoming visible as he stepped into the light. One of his bikini babes followed him, a thong sticking in her butt crack and an uzi strapped around her shoulder. He came up to Lillith, taking her hand and, just as he was about to kiss it he looked her in the eyes, saying, "How I've missed you, Lillith." Then he kissed her hand.

"You're too kind." Lillith withdrew her hand and stood, addressing everyone. "I've asked you here to show you a new technology I've had developed." She took a vial of blue liquid and held it forth. "This little container holds enough genetically engineered DNA to turn 20 normal foot-soldiers into unstoppable beasts."

Mastermind raised his eyebrow in interest. Vinny squinted, clenching his fists and The Dragon Lady remained composed, as always.

Lillith took a hypo-needle and inserted the vial. She turned to her minion, saying, "Come closer." He squirmed, whimpering as he inched towards her until Lillith took him by the wrist and inserted the needle into his arm.

Bemused, he rubbed the spot where he'd been injected. Lillith took a step backward as the minion convulsed, dropping to the floor and curling up on his side. He dry-heaved so hard his lungs might have come out and his eyes bulged, turning red. Still convulsing, his arms and legs began to bulge, his muscles growing until they ripped through his bondage slave suit, seeming as if they would rip out of his skin. Bones protruded from his back, his spine lengthening. Finally, green vomit spewed from his mouth and with it, a primal roar.

He stood, grabbing a nearby metal barrel and crushing it with his deformed hands. He threw the crushed barrel across the room then turned to Lillith, who cooed sweetly in his ear as he pawed at her.

Vinny stepped backwards, "This ain't right!" He looked to his left, and to his right, to the others. "This isn't natural! I'm leaving, Lillith." He walked off, his bodyguard following while still gazing in shock at the man-beast.

"Very well," said Lillith. "How about you, Mastermind?"

"I must have it, Lillith. I'll stop at nothing."

Lillith could tell he was lying, but his feigned interest was still useful. She turned to The Dragon Lady, "And you?"

"I would be interested to see what are the side-effects. Perhaps you could provide a small sample? For testing."

Mastermind interjected, "No need for that, I'll buy your entire stock. Name your price."

Lillith replied, "Twenty million for twenty vials."

"Done. But I have one condition, the vials must be delivered to my lair by you, personally."

Lillith knew he was up to something, but she agreed and, turning to The Dragon Lady, she bowed her head, saying, "Thank you for your interest."

The Dragon Lady returned the bow, saying nothing, and withdrew with her bodyguard from the room.

Suzuki somersaulted past the air vent, landing on her feet like a black cat. Her ninja robes blended into the night and she leapt onto the ledge, stopping to look nine stories down from atop the roof of the hotel. A car went by on the street.

She attached the hook on the end of her rope to the building and leaned out, rappelling down the side until she was on a porch protruding from a room on the fifth floor.

The sliding glass door was open, drapes flowing out of it with the breeze. The lights were out, and she could hear snoring. She unsheathed the katana strapped to her back, stepping through the door and standing next to the bed.

Stabbing downward, her sword pierced a pillow and lodged into the mattress. The lights flicked on, and she looked to see Martin standing by the bathroom just as he shot lightning bolts into her. She flew backwards, into the wall, and fell in a heap on the floor. Just as she was opening her eyes a fist slammed into her temple.

Martin stood over her unconscious body, then took a rope and tied her hands and feet.

He went over to the bed, pulling the covers away to reveal a small tape recorder which was playing the sound of him snoring from the night before. He pressed a button and it stopped.

These were the moments Lilly dreaded, alone in a motel room with nothing to do but think. She lay in bed, fully clothed and over the covers. Dan was chatting up a waitress at the counter of a nearby diner and Barry was probably watching a titty flick in his room. She closed her eyes, hoping the memories wouldn't come, but they did. The tightness in her chest meant she was still a young girl alone in a room.

She had no idea, but it was her twelfth birthday. She rubbed the inside of her arm, which was sore from needles. She had stopped crying, and was sitting on the bed, her feet dangling just above the floor. Going over to a tray of food that had been slid through an opening in the door, she carried it back to her bed. Sitting and holding her pillow against her, she ate a piece of toast.

Jack called to her, "Lilly? Are you there?", his voice carrying through the air duct which connected her room to the one next to it. She put her tray and pillow aside, going over to the vent on the floor by the wall and sitting down next to it, holding her knees.

"Hi, Jack."

"You were gone longer than usual." His voice sounded distant and muffled as it passed through the ducts.

"They took a lot of blood. My arm hurts."

"I'm sorry to hear that."

"I been thinking, Jack. Someday we're going to escape this place and live somewhere together. Somewhere nice."

There was a long pause. Lilly asked if he was still there. He replied, "Listen to me Lilly. When you see a chance to escape, take it, and don't look back. Forget everything else. You hear me?"

She wanted to cry, but instead she answered, "I hear you."

"I wouldn't have anywhere to live in this world anyways. Now go eat your food. I'm tired. Think I'll rest early today."

"Okay, Jack."

Lilly got herself up. Pacing by the bed a few times, she stopped, looking towards the door, then went out and walked down the hall towards Barry's room.

Women's Prison Four was just getting to the good part and I was reaching down to unzip my fly when there was a knock on the door. I rose and went over, opening the door to find Martin standing there with a limp ninja draped over his shoulder.

"Stand aside before someone sees me." He pushed past me and heaved the unconscious ninja onto the bed.

I was closing the door again when Lilly came up, pushing it open. "What's going on!?"

"Lilly, this is Martin. He's the one who brought me back when I wasn't myself."

Lilly looked at him. "What's with the ninja?"

"I've captured an enemy agent. You ever heard of XenoCore Genetics Labs? Its where we're going. Lillith's plans involve some experiments they've been doing in secret."

Lilly lowered her gaze. "I've heard of them. And I already knew that." She went over to the agent, looking down at her. "You remember to get rid of her me-phone?"

Martin replied, "She has a me-phone?"

Lilly started patting her down, "Fuck!" She found the me-phone and threw it on the ground, stomping it with her heel.

"Who can keep up with all this technology!?"

Lilly stopped him, "Shh!", and, listening intently, asked, "You hear that?"

I strained my ears. I heard it. "Its a chopper."

Lilly was already headed for the door, "Let's go! I'll get Dan. Meet me at the car."

Martin yelled after her, "What about the prisoner?"

"No time! Leave her."

Agent Penny flew the chopper, angling downward as they approached Suzuki's signal. Tiffany manned the chain gun, pointing it out the side door with one hand and checking her me-phone with the other.

"Shit!", Tiffany screamed into her headset, "We lost the signal!"

"We're almost on top of them, keep your eyes open."

Tiffany scanned the ground, looking for them, and saw Lilly taking a weapon from the trunk of a car. "Bank right!"

Penny banked as bullets struck the windshield. She looked to see Lilly firing an AK-47 from behind a mini-van. "Blue mini-van! Light it up!"

Tiffany fired, sending a stream of bullets downward and ripping the mini-van to shreds.

"You get 'er?", Penny asked.

Tiffany looked, but couldn't see Lilly. "I think so."

Penny was looking for any signs of her when a rocket struck them from behind, the explosion shaking the chopper and nearly knocking Tiffany out the door.

"Oh fuck!", Penny yelled as the chopper spun and she struggled to maintain control. Its tail struck the top of a tree, and Penny hit the controls hard as they crash landed by the side of the freeway.

"Everyone in the car," Lilly ordered. Dan got in, starting the engine.

"Should we go finish 'em off?", I asked.

"With any luck, they're dead. We're not sticking around to find out. Let's go."

We loaded up and got in. As we pulled out of the parking lot I turned to Lilly, "Where are we going?"

"New Mexico."

Martin turned around. "That's where XenoCore is based. You have a plan?"

"I've had a plan for a long time." She stared out the window, looking to a far off place as Dan merged onto the freeway.

7

Baxter was a silverback mountain gorilla. He used his enormous arms to push a food cart slowly along the hallway, making his rounds, plodding with powerful legs. He wore a white smock over his barrel chest, stained with grease from cooking. He stopped outside Jack's room, taking a tray with canned corn and a couple potatoes and sliding it through a small opening in the door.

Jack had been waiting for him, "Thanks, Baxter."

Baxter signed the words for *You're welcome*, with his hands while simultaneously saying, "No problem, Jack," his voice deep and gravelly.

The last tray had food piled onto it. Mashed potatoes with gravy and a whole chicken with two cobs of corn on the side. Baxter lowered his gaze as he approached Sheila's room. He didn't have to slide it in, he just opened the door because Sheila liked it there, and the scientists had granted her privileges.

He found her lounging naked on a settee, slurping a strawberry milkshake from a straw. Her folds of fat poured over the side of the couch and a reality show played on a large screen high definition TV, blaring loudly.

She threw the milkshake at him, and Baxter winced as it bounced off his shoulder, pink milkshake splashing onto his fur.

"About time! I gave birth to twins today, so I get a chicken!"

Baxter carried her food tray over as she reached out, gesturing with her fingers greedily until she grabbed it and set it on her mountain of a belly, tearing off a leg and stuffing her mouth with greasy meat.

With her mouth full she glared at him, mumbling, "Get lost monkey!"

Baxter turned and pushed the cart out of the room.

Returning to the kitchen, he cleaned pans and wiped down the counter. As he went into the walk-in pantry to put away some spices he heard Randy, the new employee, enter the kitchen with Donna, one of the lab techs. Unseen, he listened.

"Forget Mandy, baby. I'm breaking it off with her

first chance I get. I need a real woman like you."

"I don't know, Randy. I like you, but I don't think I should."

"Listen, I just closed a deal with the North Koreans. Let's celebrate tonight. Just dinner at my place, some wine and food. What's wrong with that?"

Baxter came out of the pantry, clearing his throat. "Excuse me, I was just cleaning up."

Randy lowered his hand which he had been resting on the wall next to Donna's head. He adjusted the coat of his tailored suit and leaned in to speak softly to her, "Head back to the lab, baby, I'll see you later."

She left, and Randy turned to Baxter. "Sneaking around again, Baxter? You know you'd better keep this to yourself."

"Keep what to myself? Its none of my concern."

"That's a good monkey." He went over to a tray of scones on the counter, taking one and biting off a piece. "These are really good!" He turned away and walked out of the kitchen, leaving Baxter alone.

I don't know what it was, but I was starting to hope I had a chance with Lilly. That night in a motel I stayed awake, thinking about her and when I awoke in the morning she was still on my mind. I shook it off, going to get a little styrofoam bowl full of cereal-os. She came in, sitting down across from me with an instant coffee, eating her waffle, her eyes still droopy from sleep.

Normally I would have told her she looked crappy, because she did, but, somehow I said, "You look great."

Still chewing a piece of waffle she looked at me like I was crazy. "What's wrong with you?"

"Nothing's wrong, you just look better than you normally would." I gritted my teeth. I hadn't wanted to say that.

"And you look like a butt has been grafted onto your stupid face!" She picked up her plate and cup and went to the table across the room.

I sucked it up, letting her sit with a middle-aged couple from Arkansas. I'd apologize later, if I felt like it.

Martin had been getting cereal, and he took her seat at my table. "Forget any ideas you have about Lilly."

"Why would I do that?"

"She's too good for you. She's special and you're not." He poured his milk. "Let me tell you a story. Long ago, god it feels like a lifetime, I was in the clutches of Lillith. She had me tied down on a mattress in a dark basement somewhere, my hands tied to the wall above my head. Every day one of her agents would come into my room, taunting me, stimulating me, but never allowing me to climax. The blue balls lasted days. Then weeks."

I stopped chewing. "That's awful."

"The pain was beyond unbearable, and, at first I was afraid I was losing my mind. Then I stopped being afraid. What happened next is hazy, like a dream, but, when I was beyond help, Lillith came to me, and she released me, telling me that our child would someday kill me. She handed me a knife and said I should cut off my balls. So I did. When I awoke, I was in an alleyway somewhere in Morocco."

"Ouch! That's the worst story ever." Then it dawned on me, "You're not telling me that Lilly..."

"I wasn't sure, but now I'm certain. Yes." He took a mouthful of cereal, speaking as he chewed, "If you hurt her, and don't take this the wrong way, but I believe I will kill you."

I'd heard the old protective father shtick before, but it was odd hearing it come from Martin. I looked over to see Lilly staring out the window, moving what was left of her waffle around her plate with a fork. "Does she know?"

He laughed, nearly spitting out his food. "I'm sure she doesn't. And I'm sure she doesn't care to." He put his finger over his lips as he said this and then left the table, leaving his plate where it was.

I got up and went over to her. "Hey, Lilly, I just wanted to say that I'm sorry for what I said."

"Nevermind." She got up, tossing her plate into the

trash. "We gotta' hit the road if we're gonna' make Santa Fe by Friday. Tell everyone to get ready." With that, she went off to her room to gather her stuff.

We merged onto the highway and settled in for a long journey. We hit Texas around noon, its flat landscape adding to the monotony, and each hour faded into the next.

That afternoon, somewhere outside of Dallas, we passed an amusement park. Lilly yelled, "Stop! Pull over," and Dan pulled to the side of the highway. Lilly got out of the car, standing there, gazing at the park with its roller coasters rising into the sky.

I got out and stood next to her. She just stood, saying nothing. "Its Magic Land, Lilly. You never seen it before?"

"Not in person."

Martin came up behind us and, seeing Lilly's fascination he said, "There's always time for a little magic in our lives. What say we spend a few hours here?"

"Alright with me," I said. I wasn't in any hurry.

"Yes." Lilly returned to the car, hurrying.

Mastermind's lair was inside a volcano on a small island off the coast of Malaysia. Lillith was making the last leg of her journey, riding one of his helicopters. The pilot was a bikini babe, and she spoke little, so Lillith just kept to herself, her hands snugly over the case containing the vials.

The pilot took them over the smoking mouth of the volcano and down into it. They landed on an expansive platform which jutted out from the rock and Lillith stepped out before the helicopter flew into the air again, chopping the sulfuric smoke which rose from deep beneath them. There was a metal door in the rock itself with two bikini babes strapped with uzis guarding it. Lillith stepped over and placed the case on the platform. One of the bikini babes spoke up, "Welcome to Mastermind's lair, he's waiting inside." She reached over and tapped a code into the electronic lock, and the door slid open. "Please follow me."

Lillith picked up her case and followed the bikini babe into an elevator. The bikini babe pressed the button on the bottom of the row and the door slid shut.

They stood in silence as the elevator descended. The indicator above the door cycled downward through twenty two floors until it reached the bottom, and when the door opened the bikini babe remained standing, simply gesturing with her arm for Lillith to proceed.

Lillith stepped out onto a metal walkway, and looked into an enormous cavern. Lights illuminated the stalactites above her and she peered over the railing, looking downward into what seemed an endless abyss.

"There's no safer place in the world." She turned to see Mastermind coming up some stairs.

"I'm not worried about it, Mastermind, but I think I'll keep hold of this railing, just in case."

Mastermind waved her over to him, "Come. Follow me, I have something to show you."

Lillith followed him down the steps until they came to another platform beside a large door. As Mastermind keyed in the code to open it he said, "Very few have seen what you're about to."

The door slid to the side, revealing a large natural cavern with a giant video screen rising to the ceiling on its far wall. It displayed current news footage as well as feeds from surveillance cameras all over the world. Each moving image had its own little section on which it was displayed, and, from the back of the cavern, the entire screen looked like a bricolage of visual information.

Mastermind went over to sit in a metal chair with buttons and switches on the armrests with which he could control every detail of his subterranean volcano lair. "I noticed you've been having difficulty with a certain small group."

Lillith remained silent.

"Come now, not to worry. I'm here to help."

The glow from the giant screen moved over the white skin on his bald head and his face, and danced over the stalactites jutting down from the top of the cavern. His eyes darted from place to place, following his curiosity towards whatever image struck him as relevant. "Now where was that feed I saw earlier, ah yes!"

He pressed a button and the entire screen showed Lilly, Martin, Barry and Dan standing in line at Magic Land.

Lillith broke her silence, "Why are you doing this?"

"We'll get to that later, but for now just let your people know where they are. Don't worry, we get excellent reception down here."

Lillith took her me-phone and dialed.

We pulled into Magic Land and got into line at the entrance. Lilly kept popping up on her toes to see, over the heads of people in Magic Mouse hats with their big blue ears, how far the line into the park went. After a while we purchased four tickets and pushed our way through the turnstiles. Lilly hurried forward, "I'm going on the Death Spiral first."

We had to pick up our pace to keep up with her, past people in elephant and penguin suits, as she made her way to the Death Spiral. I looked up to see the loops of the roller coaster towering above us. Martin turned to me, "Anyone ever fall off this thing?"

Dan said wryly, "Not very often."

"You'll most likely live," I told him, and he checked the loops again as people zoomed around it in the cars, yelling and screaming.

"That's comforting."

Lilly got into the front car, and I sat next to her, pulling the safety bars down over our laps. Dan and Martin got in behind us. The cars moved forward, pulled by a chain in the tracks, and we came out into the open, curving right. Climbing upwards to the top of the big hill, I looked around at all the people below. They looked tiny, scurrying around the buildings. There were clouds on the horizon, and it was beautiful.

Lilly gripped the bar tight, white knuckled, and we lurched over the top of the hill, falling. My stomach seemed to lift into my chest and, for the briefest moment, I felt I was flying. Reaching the bottom we soared upwards again and into the first loop, the cars shaking as we turned upside down. I yelled and I could see glimpses of people down there, over my head. We came through the loop and flew up another hill, and I looked over to see a giant smile on Lilly's face as she laughed, wind whipping through her hair as she braced for another loop.

When the ride was over we pulled into the loading area. The bars lifted and Lilly jumped out, "Let's go again!"

Martin stepped out of his car and stumbled towards the exit. He stopped and, leaning forward and heaving, puked onto the floor. He turned to Lilly, wiping vomit from his mouth. "There's plenty of other rides to go on, Lilly. Let's try the Wild Mushroom Ride."

We got in line for the Mushroom Ride. A giant plastic mountain towered above us with brightly colored mushrooms painted all over it. A waterfall flowed out of an opening near the top, and people riding in fake logs went over it, falling to the bottom and getting drenched in a huge splash.

The line hadn't moved much when I saw Ronda Rottweiler get in line behind us. I couldn't believe it. She was the heavyweight women's champion cage fighter and she was enormous. The people near her started to make a fuss, and she took out a stack of head shots, signing them for everyone.

I turned to Lilly, "Hey that's Ronda Rottweiler, I'll be right back." I went over, pushing through the crowd which had gathered around her. Finally I got near her and said, "I'm a big fan Ms. Rottweiler, can I get an autograph?"

She looked at me and snarled, which took me by surprise, before writing on a picture and handing it to me. I pushed my way back to where Lilly and the rest had been holding my place in line.

Lilly asked, "What'd she write?"

I looked, and it read:

'You won't leave this place alive.

Sincerely,

Ronda

C.U.N.T.'

We had reached the front of the line and Dan and Martin were already getting in. Lilly grabbed my arm, pulling me towards them. "Come on, we'll get off in the middle of the ride."

We got in the back log, and the bars came down over our laps as Ronda pushed her way through the line. She shoved the people getting in the front log aside, saying, "I'm next!", and got in.

The water carried us away and into the mountain.

'When this life

makes you feel

Like you can't

really deal

Simply ask

with a squeal

What is real

What is real

What is real?'

We floated through a cavern full of slowly moving squirrels and rabbits among purple mushrooms as they sung in chorus a super catchy tune with their high pitched voices, looping endlessly.

"Oh man, this is gonna' suck hard," I said. I heard the sound of metal bending, and I looked to see Ronda as she snapped the safety bar and stood up, turning around to face us.

Me and Lilly pulled at the bar over our laps, trying in vain to get it to budge. Ronda jumped onto the next log over, stepping through the frightened people, past Dan and Martin, who were still unsure what was happening, and making her way towards us. I kept yanking at the bar as Lilly squirmed sideways and slipped out from under it, standing to face Ronda as she jumped onto the log in front of ours.

The log bobbed and swayed in the water as Lilly stepped forward. We emerged into the next cavern where more small woodland creatures were still singing. Ronda leaped onto our log and Lilly kicked at her legs, sending her falling forward. Ronda's face was right in front of mine, and I stopped pulling on the bar to punch her in the face. She grinned through her teeth and growled at me. Lilly grabbed around her back as she stood, clinging to her. Ronda took the time to lift her boot and kick me in the teeth.

I saw lights, my head snapping backwards. By the time I could see straight again Ronda was on top of Lilly, strangling her and grunting. I forced my legs sideways, slipping my knees from under the bar, and I was able to lift it just enough to get free. I stood and stepped forward, leaping over to the next log and standing behind them.

I slammed my fist into the back of Ronda's head, and she let go of Lilly to turn around and swing at me. I ducked, her fist catching air, and I leaned in to tackle her with my shoulder. We flew off the log, landing next to a pink dancing bear.

I rolled to my side and got to my feet, facing Ronda, who had her hands up by her face, circling me, looking for an opening. I leaned in and tried to punch, but she dove for my legs, shooting in and grabbing them, and lifting me into the air before slamming me on my back. She straddled me and I curled up as fist after fist slammed into my face.

My head struck the floor with each hit, and I panicked, shielding myself in vain.

I felt a jolt of electricity, shocking me, and Ronda yelled out. I opened my eyes as Ronda got up off me, and I saw Lilly there, holding a broken electrical cable. Ronda turned and when she stepped away from me Lilly thrust the end of the cable into her belly. Ronda went stiff, her eyes bulging as electricity convulsed her.

The animals dancing around the room and the song

they were singing went faster and faster, the song rising to a high pitched squeal, the torsos swinging, and the little furry arms going up and down in a blur. Circuits blew and sparks exploded everywhere and, after a while, Ronda's body, still frozen in place, stiffened.

Lilly withdrew the cable, and all the animals slowed to a standstill, the song whirring into silence as the lights in the cavern went dark. Ronda slumped to the floor, falling dead.

"You okay?" Lilly helped me to my feet.

My face was messed up, and I tried to look stoic. I touched my lip. "Ouch!"

Lilly helped me forward. "Come on, let's find an exit before security comes."

We found Martin and Dan outside the Wild Mushroom Ride and we all left the park in a hurry, making our way to the car. We pulled onto the highway, headed west.

I sat in the back seat next to Lilly, and I could see that she was distraught over the whole situation. Then she started crying, hands over her face, sobbing and heaving.

I put my arm around her, saying, "Its okay."

"Its not okay!" She yelled in between sobs, then caught her breath. She said angrily, "I shouldn't have stopped there! I should have just kept going to Santa Fe. I nearly got killed and Jack would have been stuck in that lab forever."

She kept crying, more softly now, and I held her close. "Its going to be okay," I said. "We'll get your friend out."

8

Mastermind had hoped that Lillith's assassin would be successful so that she'd be in a good mood when he asked her his question. When her woman died, the video feed cutting out as she was fried by an electrical cable, he had suggested to Lillith that she rest in one of his spare bedrooms. She agreed, and Mastermind sat alone trying to figure out how best to approach her.

He realized that delaying wouldn't help, so he rose from his chair and, taking a deep breath, walked out of his vid-chamber towards Lillith's room. Outside the door he lifted his fist to knock, but hesitated. Lillith was notoriously cruel. What if she laughed at him? Or worse, treated him with scorn? A little voice in his head said to him, '*Grab your balls, Mastermind. There's no going back.*' He knocked.

He stood, waiting with his arms stiff by his side until the door opened and Lillith stood before him. She greeted him, "Well, hello."

He began to speak, "Lillith, I..." He stopped, then asked if he could come in.

"Of course." Lillith stood aside and he entered.

He stopped in the middle of the room, turning to face her. He said, "I hope the room is adequate."

"More than adequate."

"Good, good." He rolled back and forth on his feet, his hands behind his back, looking around the room. "The cave is heated naturally from the magma pools far below."

"Yes, I had assumed that was the case."

He stammered, "Lillith... I want to ask you something."

"Go ahead."

"You've been around a long time, over five thousand years." He laughed nervously. "So I'm sure you know a thing or two about..." He stopped mid-sentence, then continued, "You know something about women."

She giggled. "I should hope so, I am one after all."

"Yes, and I've been thinking a lot about having an heir to take over, you know, after I die, but..."

Lillith was seeing where this was headed. "You're

having trouble finding a mate, is that it?"

He laughed in relief, "Yes. Lillith, how do I get women to like me?"

"You don't."

Mastermind was stymied, "What do you mean?"

"The best a man can do is learn to be himself, if a woman likes you, she likes you and if she doesn't, its totally beyond your concern. You're a very smart man, Mastermind, but, please, don't fall into the trap of believing that you can control a woman or manipulate her into liking you. Most often, its actually the women who allow the men to believe they're in control. Its women's most powerful strategy and the reason we secretly rule the world."

Mastermind smiled in understanding, "Yes, I see. Thank you Lillith."

"Don't mention it."

We rented a van and set it up with surveillance equipment, parking it along the street not far from Xenocore Labs, which was located just outside Santa Fe where the hills begin to rise. Taking turns, we watched and listened as employees went in and out, making notes of times and persons as we studied the routines of all the goings on.

When not manning the surveillance van we stayed in a nearby hotel, resting and going over our part in the plan with Lilly.

The night before the plan was to be executed I lay in bed, going over and over it in my head until I fell asleep.

I dreamt that night about a cabin up in the hills, surrounded by forest. I was chopping wood, and then Lilly came out from the cabin, holding a tray of severed fingers. At 5:30 AM the alarm blared, rousting me into wakefulness.

I rose, dressing in my janitor clothes and went out, knocking on Lilly's door.

"Hold on!" I heard her yelling, "I'm on the toilet." I waited, getting fidgety. I didn't want to stop and think about today. Finally I heard the toilet flush and she came and opened the door. "Come in."

As I entered she asked me, "You ready?"

I took a deep breath. "Yeah."

"Let's get everything into the van. Martin and Dan are already downstairs."

We waited in the van across from Xenocore Labs. Dan was posted down the street, and when the janitor drove by him he signaled us.

I took a series of quick deep breaths, holding my

pistol, and Lilly slid open the door. I stepped out, walking quickly across the street as the janitor pulled into the parking lot. I made for the spot where he always parked, and just as he pulled in I raised my pistol.

He looked at me as I continued towards him and, just as I was about to fire he flung open the car door and knocked the pistol out of my hand. He reached down to grab it off of the concrete, and I slammed the door onto his arm, sending the pistol sliding under the car. I opened the door again and swung at him, hitting him on the side of his head. I pushed him over, getting on him and wrapping my fingers around his throat, squeezing, grunting.

Another car pulled into the spot next to us, and through the window I could see her gasp, and pull away again while she grabbed her me-phone. I punched the janitor in the temple, and he was dazed just enough for me to get out and reach under the car for the pistol. I felt it with my fingers, scooching it towards me, then grabbed it and rolled my body, aiming at the other employee's car and firing repeatedly through her rear windshield.

I hit her in the head, sending blood spatter across her interior, and her car rolled into a light post.

The janitor was getting out when I turned and shot him in the chest.

I heard gunfire coming from the labs main entrance, and a shot ricocheted off the door next to me. I crouched down, returning fire and the two guards hid behind a bush.

Lilly came running across the road, firing her AK-47 and ran right up to them, shooting them down and running in the door. I ran, following her inside.

A woman was running through the lobby and Lilly shot her down. She ran over and ripped the pass card off her white lab coat. She turned to me, "Let's go!"

Martin ran up to us, "I'm going too, Lilly!"

We came up to the high security door, and Lilly swiped the card. The door unlocked and we went through.

Lilly ran down the hallway, stopping before the second to last door on the right. She yelled, "Jack! Can you hear me?"

"Lilly? Is that you?"

"Stand back Jack, I'm shooting the lock."

She fired into the door lock, shredding it, and the door swung loose. Lilly went in and we followed.

I'm not sure how, but when I saw Jack, I wasn't all that surprised to see an alien, gray skin, big round head, just like in the movies. He was crouched in the far corner, long slim arms wrapped around himself and he hid his face as Lilly came up to him. "Lilly, don't look at me."

Lilly took a vial of that blue stuff she had injected

me with and gave Jack a shot of it in his arm. "This should help you get your strength back."

Jack drew a long breath, feeling the effects of the shot. He turned his head, regarding Lilly, who looked back at him in love and recognition. "You knew?"

"Yes, I always knew. Can you walk? We need to go."

Martin approached and, with Lilly, took his arms to help him up. They helped him forward, towards the door.

I opened it, standing aside for them, only to see Lillith, with her pointy spectacles and white beehive hair-do, standing there holding a gun.

Lillith fired, and Martin, yelling, jumped in front of Lilly. He fell to his knees, holding the bleeding wound in his chest.

Lillith giggled, still pointing her smoking gun. "Well, well, Martin. I told you our child would kill you someday."

"Lillith, you always were a royal cunt." He coughed blood, and looked up at Lilly, trying to speak, "Lilly...", but weakness overtook him and he slumped to the floor.

A beastly roar bellowed from down the hall. Lillith turned to see, and went white with fear as Baxter bounded along towards her, slamming his giant arms against her little body and sending her flying into the door at the end of the hall. I went to look, seeing her crumpled on the ground.

"Thank you, Baxter," Lilly told him.

Baxter signed, "You're welcome." He came up to her, giving her a hug with his enormous arms, being careful not to crush her. He said, "Can I come too, Lilly?"

"Yes, carry Jack. We're getting out of here."

Baxter lifted Jack, holding him under one arm as Lilly leaned down and put a hand on Martin's shoulder, who lay face down in a pool of blood. She checked his pulse, finding he was dead. "Thank you," she whispered softly to him.

We left the room and I looked to see that Lillith was missing and the door that she had slammed against was open. There was an emergency exit nearby.

Baxter said, "Sheila must have taken her."

"Nevermind. Let's go."

We hurried out of Xenocore Labs. Dan had the van parked just outside and we piled in, slamming the door shut as we peeled away.

9

We made our way north into Colorado, where we had secured a cabin in the mountains, well away from anyone. The mountain road turned into a dirt road and we turned again, following what seemed no more than a trail.

Pulling up to the cabin, which sat at one end of a large meadow, we got out, stretching our achy limbs. I looked around to see forested hills and mountain peaks to the west. Lilly and the others went inside, Jack now walking without Baxter's help, but I lingered, sitting myself on the front deck, taking it all in. I thought to myself, everything is so beautiful here, and just knowing that it would never last made me long for a place, somewhere to rest and be safe.

I shook it off, getting to my feet. I went to the van and grabbed the AK-47, yelling to Lilly, who was standing in the door, that I needed to go look around, and maybe shoot some dinner or something.

I hiked through the woods, following the contours between the ridges of the mountains until I came across a stream. I followed the stream, higher into the mountains, then cut north to climb one of the peaks.

I scrambled and clung to rocks until I stood at the top, and I stood looking out across the landscape. Wind swept over the trees and dark clouds were forming on the horizon. It looked like rain was coming, but I didn't care. I had to keep going. I climbed down the other side of the peak, deeper into the wild.

Scrambling between two ridges I heard thunder, and rain began to pelt me. The sun was going down, and soon it would be dark. I kept going for a while, the ground becoming soaked and my clothes drenched, until I found a small cave in the side of a hill. In the shadow of a peak I climbed up to it, and crawled inside, curling up against the rock wall and listening to the storm raging just outside until, after awhile, I drifted into sleep.

Lilly had a can of beans cooking on the stove top. The fire kept the cabin warm as heavy rain pelted the windows, wind whipped the trees outside, and the occasional peal of thunder reminded her how good it was to be in here.

Barry hadn't returned, but she wasn't too worried. He seemed like he just needed to be alone for awhile, and he probably got stuck by the storm, and was riding it out until it passed.

We had stopped at a Radio Hut on the way here to get all kinds of electronics for Jack. He sat at a desk, soldering pieces together. A small satellite dish lay on the ground next to him, and circuit boards, conductors, capacitors, resistors, and wires all lay haphazardly around him with more piled inside a box at his feet. A single large crystal of pure quartz sat on the desk.

Dan was already asleep on the couch, and Baxter was in the corner playing Scribble on Lilly's phone. She poured beans into three bowls and took one over to Jack and one to Baxter, and sitting herself in a lounge chair she ate her beans until, setting her bowl aside, she closed her eyes and slept.

The sun was up when I was awakened by something making noise outside the cave. I crawled to the opening, looking out to see a feral pig down the slope, snorting and huffing as it dug its snout into the dirt.

The rain had stopped and the sky was clear, but the ground was still wet. I raised my AK-47, aiming at the pig, but it shuffled behind a boulder, so I got up to climb along the rock face to get a clear shot. My foot slipped and I slid, sending dirt and rocks tumbling down the slope. The pig squealed and ran, heading down hill between the ridges.

I managed to stop my slide by bracing my feet against a rock. I righted myself and jumped onto a boulder further down before jumping again to the bottom of the slope.

I aimed at the pig, which was running through some thickets and fired, hitting a rock next to it. It kept going, around the end of the ridge and out of sight.

I ran after it, following the sound of its grunts and squeals. I leapt from rock to rock, dodging trees as I went. Stopping next to a boulder I saw it heading for the stream, and I fired another shot, missing again.

I hurried over to where it had disappeared into the trees. I stood at the top of a waterfall and, looking down, I saw its tracks left in the soft mud of the stream's bank.

I climbed down and followed the tracks as they led along the water. The pig was large and left traces of its passing at every bush until, after about a quarter of a mile I saw its tracks lead away from the stream and into the trees.

I followed through the trees, broken branches and footprints leading to a meadow. I crouched down, looking across the clearing and listening intently.

I heard grunts. I gripped my gun tight, not moving. I waited, watching, and the pig emerged from some bushes at the other end of the clearing.

I raised my AK-47 slowly, aiming carefully. The pig stood snuffling its nose in the air as I looked down the sights, and I held my breath, squeezing the trigger.

The shot rang out and with a loud squeal the pig's rear legs buckled, and it fell before getting up and trying to run into the trees, but its body fell sideways, and it lay down, squealing and dying on the ground.

I stepped out from the bushes and into the meadow, making a fist and crying out, "Yeah! I got you bitch!"

My voice echoed through the mountains, 'YOU BITCH!', 'You Bitch!', 'you bitch!'.

Someone screeched from behind me, through the trees. Then another screech to my left. As I looked around I heard shouts and high pitched cries which seemed to come from everywhere.

Two millennials stepped into the clearing, across the meadow. Both were in tight jeans, with one wearing an obscure DIY band shirt and another wearing a Captain USA t-shirt. They pointed at me, holding their me-phones, and shouted shrill cries to the others.

More millennials emerged from the trees, and I retreated away from the clearing, into cover. I heard leaves and twigs being trampled as millenials ran towards me through the woods, and I ran.

Jack had been up all night putting together his contraption. It looked like a piece of art made from garbage; old laptops, the insides of a television, a car battery and a walkie-talkie. The small satellite dish pointed upwards to the sky.

Baxter carried it outside, laying it on the grass. Lilly watched as Jack took the quartz crystal and slid it into a slot, and it glowed, shining white light.

Jack looked at Lilly and shrugged. "We'll know if its working within the hour."

Lilly wasn't too confident that the mangled mass of things would work. She went over and hugged him. "If it doesn't work, you know you can stay here with us."

"Don't be fooled by its appearance, Lilly. The parts may be primitive, but an understanding of interstellar physics is to me what common sense is to humans."

"Okay, Einstein. We'll see."

A cloud started swirling in the sky directly above us. It became a funnel, the thin part stretching down towards the ground, and a small craft, circular and spinning with lights on its edge, descended through the cloud.

Jack smiled. "Well, it worked."

Lilly began to cry. She wanted to say something. The one who had been her only friend was leaving, and it was happening right now.

Jack said, "Lilly, you're stronger than you know. Thank you for being my friend all these years."

A column of light beamed down from the craft, encompassing Jack and, as he waved to them, he lifted into the air and rose up and inside it.

It lingered just a moment, then whizzed high into the sky and disappeared.

Lilly just had time to wipe her tears away when she heard gunshots from the woods.

"What's that?" Lilly ran for the van, getting the shotgun and two handguns. "Baxter! Inside."

Baxter lumbered in through the door as Lilly turned to aim her shotgun. She saw Barry emerge, firing the AK-47 as he went, hitting a millennial in the head, his brains coming out his skull as he fell.

Dozens were converging on him as he ran across the meadow. She aimed, and fired, hitting a girl who was taking a video on her me-phone as she ran.

As Barry ran past Lilly he yelled out, "Get inside! There's too many of 'em."

Barry ran up to the door and turned, popping bullets into the nearest millennials, and Lilly backed up, pumping shells and firing as she went. Bodies fell, littering the front of the cabin.

Barry went inside, and as Lilly backed in, he fired another round and kicked the door shut, sliding the wooden plank into place to keep it closed.

Millennials slammed into the door, screaming wildly, but the door held in place.

Dan came running over, holding a handgun. "What the hell is happening?"

Barry checked the windows. "Some millennials overheard me using the 'B' word."

"Oh, fuck."

A fist shattered the side window, a millennial reaching in with a me-phone and berating us. Lilly stepped over and shot him in the face, turning it into something like raw burger.

It went quiet. Barry listened a moment, hearing nothing, and looked outside to see the millennials retreating and gathering to encircle the cabin.

Barry went over to the spare ammo and switched magazines. "They're gonna' wait us out. Smart, its what I would do. How are we on supplies?"

Lilly checked out the window. The millennials were sitting at intervals and surrounding the cabin about a hundred yards out. "We got enough food for a few days, but I don't know about water."

"Okay, we'll worry about that when the time comes. Its gonna' be a long wait." Barry opened up the sofa bed. "So let's take turns on watch. You're first, Dan, the rest of us will get some shut eye. Wake me up in a few hours."

I settled into bed, still holding my AK-47, and shut my eyes. I nodded off for a while and, just as it was getting dark, a loud bellow from outside woke me up, making me snap to attention. I jumped outta' bed and ran over to the window where Dan was watching out.

He was peering in amazement at something emerging from the trees. "What the hell is that?!"

I pushed him aside. "Lemme' see."

I saw a giant naked man, musta' been eight or nine feet tall, with orange hair, running into the clearing. Roaring, he grabbed two millennials, shaking one and banging him into the ground like a club, then tossing him and taking hold of a girl by her legs and pulling apart until they came off.

The millennials had started some fires around the cabin, and some of them grabbed burning sticks to go after the giant with, swinging the red hot embers at him. A burning stick hit him on his arm, but he just swiped at the millennial who had swung it and he went flying.

He lumbered through a group of them, swinging as he went, and sending millennials through the air until they broke, running away into the woods.

We stayed quiet, waiting to see what the giant man would do next. He looked around, seeing that all the millennials had run away, and started to whimper. He scratched his head, plopping down to sit on the ground and crying, holding his hands over his eyes.

It was pitiful, and although I felt kinda' bad, I didn't want him hanging out there. "What do we do?", I asked.

Baxter came over and looked out. "Maybe we

should see what's the matter?"

"Baxter's right," Lilly said as she slid the board out from the door. "We can't just sit here."

She opened the door, stepping out, and she approached him, going slowly with her hands out in a calming gesture.

The giant man noticed Lilly coming towards him, and with a grunt he got to his feet, taking a step backwards as if to run away, but Lilly made some soothing sounds and he stopped, unsure if he should stay or go.

Lilly approached carefully, "Hey there, big guy. Its okay, don't be afraid."

The giant man said, "Friend?"

"Yes. I'm your friend now. Okay?"

He put out his arms towards her, saying, "Hug?"

"Okay. You want a hug? Okay."

As Lilly stepped to him a shot rang out, and a bullet struck the giant man in the head, snapping it to the side as he fell to the ground.

Lilly yelled, "What the fuck, Barry?!"

Barry ran out to her, "Are you okay?"

"You fucking shot him!"

Barry stopped moving. "He was trying to grab you! I was keeping you safe!"

"I was getting through to him, Barry!"

Dan emerged from the cabin, holding his phone. "Hey guys!"

They stopped arguing, both looking at Dan, and he continued, "I just got off the phone with my people at the Mossad. They've located Lillith."

10

We chartered a jet, Dan piloting, flying us out of Denver to head for Israel where we would hook up with the Mossad. On the way we made a detour to land at an airstrip near the jungly mountains of the Congo.

Baxter had made it clear he wished to return to his homeland and teach his fellow gorillas to speak. We gently questioned his plans, but he was determined to bring the mountain gorillas up by educating them in the ways of communication, so we said goodbye to him as we stood on the airfield, his backpack full of bananas and a tablet loaded with the entire hooked-into-phonics lesson series.

Taking off again we flew to Israel, and embarked

on two weeks preparation for the mission. Lillith had been located on a volcanic island off the coast of Malaysia, in the lair of an evil genius named Mastermind. Dan was put in charge of two teams of ten men each, and Lilly and myself would be on team one.

Our two helicopters landed on an Israeli frigate near Malaysia. We got into two small boats, everyone loaded up with tactical gear, and motored over the waves towards shore. The volcano rose into the sky ahead of us, surrounded by jungle, plumes of gas rising from its mouth, and as the boats hit the sand everyone jumped out and pulled them onto shore.

We gathered, kneeling on the beach as Dan ordered the men to split up into two groups and make their way, single file, through the jungle towards a supply entrance near the base of the volcano.

I felt something squirming where my shin rested on the sand, and I checked to see as one of the men yelled out, crying in pain. He jumped to his feet and lifted his leg to find a robotic crab had pinched through his pants and was dangling from him by its pincers, its metal shell glinting in the sun.

Another metal crab squirmed its way out of the sand by my foot, and I jumped away from it, only to step on another one behind me. They were crawling out of the sand all around us.

Dan barked, "Everyone off the beach! Get to the trees!"

We ran, crabs scurrying after us. One of the men fell when a crab pinched the back of his heel, landing on other ones which pinched him with their steel pincers, not letting go.

The rest of us made it to the trees, and I used the butt of my rifle to knock one off of Dan's leg, the crab pulling a piece of flesh with it as it fell.

Dozens of crabs swarmed the man who had fallen, pinching him over and over as he flailed wildly, unable to get to his feet. He disappeared under a pile of them, and crabs pinched into his face, his eyes, his mouth, his entire body, blood spilling onto their steel shells. We could only watch as he went silent and still, covered in a writhing mass of metal.

We re-grouped, Dan ordering us to hike it through the jungle.

Mastermind stood outside Sheila's room dressed in nothing but a baby blue colored bath robe. He had been informed by Lillith that Sheila was incredibly fertile, and he thought, *what the heck, may as well get an heir*.

Sheila, already knowing what he was up to, yelled from inside her room, writhing on the bed and shouting, "Fuck me! Get in here and fuck me!"

Mastermind knocked on the door, and Sheila shouted, "Come get it!"

He opened the door, peeking his head in. Sheila lay

naked and sprawled on her back, almost lifting it off the mattress as she convulsed in fits of horniness. Her folds of fat jiggled as she writhed. "Is it alright if I come in?"

"Give it to me, Mastermind, I need it! I need it bad!"

Mastermind came up to her and reached between her legs, shutting his eyes and lifting her belly, trying to find her vagina when alarms rang, a siren blaring throughout the lair. He dropped her belly fat and checked his me-phone, which was connected to all the systems in the complex, and saw that the outer perimeter defenses had been engaged against intruders.

Without a word he ran to his control room, Sheila screaming at him as he left.

We trudged through the jungle, split into two groups. I followed right behind Lilly, who used a machete to hack at branches and thick bushes as we went.

We hadn't gone a hundred yards when someone in the other group cried out, a row of metal spikes swinging out, impaling him and pinning him to a tree.

I was just taking another step when Lilly put her arm out, stopping me. She pointed down at the ground by my feet where a red laser beam hovered just above my toes. I gingerly moved my foot away.

Dan shouted so everyone could hear, "Alright!

Everyone keep an eye out for booby traps. Keep going, single file."

I stepped over the laser beam, turning and warning the men behind me. We kept going, stepping more carefully than before.

Lillith entered the control room, where Mastermind was watching camera feeds of soldiers approaching through the jungle. She limped badly, one knee still sore from the gorilla attack, and she couldn't move her head because of a large neck brace. Her right arm was encased in a full cast.

She came up behind him, looking up at the giant wall of video screens. Mastermind zoomed in on one of the men as he was about to walk into a booby trap.

He snickered, then turned to Lillith. "I have hidden cameras all over the island. Want to see some fun?"

Lillith looked to see a man walking while gazing up at a rope net which held an old skeleton that hung from the tree above him. His eyes on the skeleton, he took another step and fell through a covering of palm leaves into a deep pit, a set of steel spikes impaling him. Mastermind giggled gleefully.

"There's still a lot of them left, Mastermind, and they're almost to the entrance. Can't you fire some missiles or something?"

"Its more fun this way! Don't worry, if any of them

make it to the volcano my bikini babes will handle them."

We'd lost over half our men by the time we made it to the supply entrance. Dan signaled us silently with his fist and we all crept into position, hiding behind trees and bushes. There were a dozen bikini babes standing guard outside a sliding metal door built into the volcano, and from his position behind a tree, Dan fired, hitting a bikini babe, mangling her perfect body.

The rest of us opened fire as the bikini babes scrambled for cover. They returned fire with their uzis but we downed most of 'em within the first twenty seconds, and then Dan tossed a grenade. It exploded, and the uzis stopped.

Dan attached some plastic explosive to the door. Taking cover, he detonated it and the explosion opened a giant hole.

We stepped through, one by one, to find a tunnel lined with concrete. It was dark, and we turned on our flashlights. We hurried forward. The floor was angled upwards and, as we went, we ascended and went deeper into the volcano.

We reached the end of the tunnel to find it opened up into a natural cave. There was a freight elevator with railings and no roof there, and with our flashlights we could see up into a natural shaft, so we got in the elevator and pressed the button.

As we ascended through the shaft we kept our guard up, rifles ready, and as we entered into a dark cavern, bikini babes started firing at us from positions on a network of metal walkways built into the rock sides. We aimed at the muzzle flashes, trying to shine our flashlights to find the shooters.

Two men went down, falling to the floor at our feet, and we returned fire. Lilly hit a bikini babe who was running along a walkway, and she fell over the railing, falling into the chasm, her picturesque curves dashing against the rock.

I hit another one, and her uzi kept firing as she convulsed in shock, hitting the bikini babe on the walkway above her.

We kept rising through the cavern, and it narrowed again into a shaft. There was a brief respite, but we looked above us to see another cavern approaching. We reloaded our weapons.

As we entered the cavern bullets struck all around us, ricocheting everywhere. Another one of our men fell and, as we returned fire, the elevator stopped.

We were pinned and taking damage. I looked to see a walkway about twenty feet down and away. I shouted, "We have to jump for it!", and I climbed, standing on the railing of the elevator. I jumped, falling, and as I saw the walkway coming towards me I braced myself and landed feet first onto it, my legs buckling as I rolled forward, and nearly falling off the end.

I got to my feet, looking for targets. I mowed one down as Lilly jumped, and when she landed next to me I grabbed her, keeping her steady.

Dan and two of our men followed as we laid down covering fire. We went along the walkway, climbing stairs and shooting.

We went up four flights of stairs and reached a wide platform. We ran across it and into a cave, going more slowly around and through stalagmites and rocks. We heard a loud growl ahead of us, and Dan raised his fist. We stopped, listening to something snarling and coming closer.

We got our rifles ready, waiting, and from around the bend a deformed bikini babe beast came at us, with its bikini top hanging ripped and torn around its rippling shoulder. We opened fire, and it stopped, flinching at the bullets, but when we had to re-load it glared at us and roared, climbing along the tunnel towards us.

It grabbed one of the men by his head, swinging him against the side of the cave, and we fired on it again. We were unloading into its back, making it wince and roar, and it turned to face us as it fell to its knees, letting out a soft yelp as it fell down dead.

Those of us that were left continued along the cave until we reached another cavern. This one was lit, and we didn't need our flashlights to see a walkway going nearly fifty yards straight across to the other side.

Someone yelled loudly from the other end, "You

want Lillith? Well, here she is!"

Mastermind held Lillith by her arm, hiding behind her. He shoved her onto the walkway and pushed her over the side. Lillith grabbed the railing with her one good hand and, dangling over an endless chasm, screamed as the man ran away, snickering as he went.

Lilly darted out onto the walkway, running across it towards Lillith. Just as her grip loosened, Lilly grabbed her hand, leaning over the railing and holding on.

Lillith pleaded in panic, "Lilly, dear Lilly. Don't let go! Don't let your mommy go!", but her hand was slipping from Lilly's grip, and she fell, screaming.

I ran up to Lilly, who gazed down into the chasm as Lillith's cries became softer and more distant, fading into silence.

I put my hand on her shoulder, saying, "Mastermind is getting away."

She looked at me, dazed, then she nodded and we all ran into the cave after him.

Soon the cave opened into a cavern with a large platform. At the edge of the platform Mastermind was sitting inside a hover-pod, its door open. He held a small device with a button, and he snickered, flipping open the plastic button cover. "Only one of us is getting out of this volcano alive!"

As the door closed and the hover-pod's jets fired, he pressed the button. There was a low thrum from deep down and the whole volcano shook.

The hover-pod rose into the air, climbing to the ceiling and disappearing into a shaft.

A rumbling grew louder, the shaking getting more intense and rocks started to fall from the sides of the cavern.

I looked around for an escape. "We gotta' get outta' here. This place is gonna' blow!"

Dan pointed. "The elevator to the top should be over that way."

We ran. Giant stalactites fell from above us, some ripping though walkways to our left and right. One hit the walkway right in front of us, mangling it. Lilly, not breaking stride, leaped across the gap. We were right behind her, and we jumped, making it across.

Dan led us to the elevator, and we pressed the button. The doors slid open and we got in, pressing the button to take us to the top.

Everything shook as we climbed, the rumble growing louder, and I actually said a little prayer to myself, in my mind, shutting my eyes in fearful fervor until the elevator reached the top. It slowed to a stop and the doors opened to the magnificent open air at the mouth of the volcano.

An Israeli chopper was hovering just above the platform, and, seeing us, it touched down. Through the grating I could see pools of lava roiling and bubbling far below as we made a dash to climb in. As the last of us boarded, the chopper lifted into the air, climbing higher as balls of molten rock spewed into the sky around us.

I looked over at Lilly, and said, "Hey, we're still alive. Right?"

She smiled. We flew over the jungle, and through the window I saw streams of lava and molten rocks flying though the air, and I leaned in, kissing her. She held my head softly in her hand, saying, "That's right."

ABOUT THE AUTHOR

I am an often uncertain man with a diagnosis of schizophrenia. One side of me is gifted, and the other is hopelessly confused. Being capable of either very little or quite a lot, I do my best, always. I've drank a chocolate milk tea every day for the last two years.